For Haley, there will never be another girl like you. Let your goodness and silliness and courage and passion lead you wherever you go. Your kind heart, your contagious laughter, and your strong and compassionate soul are what make you unrepeatably YOU.
— Frank and Carla

For Sylvia and Carolynne. The world needs girls like you.
— Kayla

Building the messages and text for this book was a collaboration that included many eyes, minds, and hearts. Many thanks to Charnaie Gordon, Amy Smith, Ro Foster, Allie Bailey, Melanie Kiker, Julie Wetherill, Dina Muncer, Theresa Mingacci, Amy Lynn, Marialena Renfro, Christine Carmen—and your sons and daughters! Leonore and Kennedi Washington, too. Christine Bailey and Barbara Dan, we hope Ava and Angelina forever see themselves on these pages. Thank you, Joe and Callie MacClay—for that powerful line. The students who helped, especially Kiley Malloy, for your inspiration. Elianna and Leslie, too. The Sedam girls, for their inspiration. The Schiavones, Bishops, and Schlemmers, too. Alice and Charlotte Lee, for your guidance. Katie Claire and Kathleen, for your support. Sarah Rockett, our editor—for your magnificent partnership. Kayla Harren for bringing radiance to our words, and Melinda Millward, for brilliant art direction. And gratitude for the entire Sleeping Bear Press team—from Julia Hlavac and Audrey Mitnick to Heather Hughes to Ben Mondloch.
— Frank and Carla

SLEEPING BEAR PRESS™
2395 South Huron Parkway, Suite 200, Ann Arbor, MI 48104
www.sleepingbearpress.com
© Sleeping Bear Press
Printed and bound in the United States.
10 9 8 7 6 5 4

Library of Congress Cataloging-in-Publication Data

Names: Murphy, Carla, author. | Murphy, Frank, author. | Harren, Kayla, illustrator.
Title: A girl like you / by Carla Murphy and Frank Murphy ; illustrated by Kayla Harren.
Description: Ann Arbor, Michigan : Sleeping Bear Press, [2020] | Audience: Ages 4-8. |
Summary: Encourages every girl to embrace all of the things that make her
unique, to be strong and kind, to stand up for herself, and more.
Identifiers: LCCN 2020007408 | ISBN 9781534110960 (hardcover)
Subjects: CYAC: Conduct of life—Fiction. | Individuality—Fiction.
Classification: LCC PZ7.1.M8714 Gir 2020 | DDC [E]—dc23
LC record available at https://lccn.loc.gov/2020007408

A GIRL like YOU

By Frank Murphy and Carla Murphy

Illustrated by Kayla Harren

PUBLISHED BY SLEEPING BEAR PRESS

There are billions and

billions

and **billions**

of people in the world.

But you are the only YOU there is!

And the world needs a girl like you.

The world needs a girl. . .

   to be strong and caring.

      To be brave and bold.

Maybe your "brave" is running for student council.

Maybe your "bold" is standing up for yourself.

Brave girl, try new things.

Find your passions.

Find your talents.

Work hard at hard things.
Mistakes are essential to success.
So stick with it.

Whether it's fixing
something that's broken,

lifting weights,
ice-skating,

or studying the moon
and the stars.

Put your mind and heart into your dreams.
And make them happen.

Sometimes you will fall.
When you do,
pick yourself up and try again.
Each time you'll become tougher and stronger!

Bold girl, speak up.

It's okay to disagree with people.

Our differences teach us about one another.

It doesn't matter how
loud or quiet,

tall or small,

fresh squeeze
for the bees

Lemonade
$2

all proceeds
go to saving
bees!

young or
old you are.

Your thoughts and opinions matter.
Be clear about how you feel.

Choose kind friends.
Friends who let *you* be YOU!
Be a kind friend too.
Take turns.
Share.

Sometimes you'll fight—that's okay.
Do say sorry when you're wrong or hurtful.
Don't make a habit of saying sorry for no reason.

When a friend is hurting, ask what they need.
You might give advice.
You might just listen.
Sometimes they'll simply need you by their side.

When a friend is proud or excited, celebrate with them.

Thoughtful girl, have empathy.

Friendships are like gardens:

tend them well and watch them grow.

Smart girl, take care of your heart.
You may feel bored or lonely or sad.

Read a good book.

Volunteer to help.

Get up early and
watch the sunrise.

Write a story. Write your story.

And if your feelings get too big—
reach out, ask for help, talk to someone who loves you.

Embrace and care for the body you are in.
Your unique traits are what make you especially beautiful.
And ESPECIALLY *you!*

What matters most is the beauty your actions
and words bring to the world.
People will remember these.
And you should too!

Radiant girl, stand tall.

Wear what feels right.
Silly socks or panda ears.

Sparkly shoes or
polka-dot pants.

A peace sign. A flag.
A flower. A rainbow.

Wear your hair up or wear your hair down.
Pigtails or ponytails.
All the way out, covered, or all the way gone.

Your clothes and hair help you express yourself.
So whatever you wear, wear it for you!

Magnificent girl, be proud.

Your smile can light up a room.

Take pride in being the one and only you.

Unlike anyone else, ever before.

And remember, the world needs a girl. . .
a caring and strong girl,
a bold and brave girl,
an unstoppable girl.

A girl like you.

Authors' Note

Whether girl, boy, or other gender identity, we know those labels come with a number of preconceptions. Children are treated differently, feel differently, and have different life experiences from those who identify as other genders. It's important that kids not feel restricted by those stereotypes. We want them to be empowered to find their passions and strengths, feel deeply, and be wholly themselves—regardless of gender.

A Girl Like You starts off with four important ideas for girls: being strong, daring, brave, and bold. We believe these are active adjectives! And one of our hopes with this book is to help empower girls to make strong, daring, brave, and bold choices—take action and live these words every day.

In addition to hoping girls make bold choices, we wanted to encourage them to make choices that serve their health—physically, mentally, and emotionally. Girls are twice as likely as boys to develop anxiety or mood disorders by the time they hit mid-adolescence. By inspiring readers to cultivate meaningful friendships and take care of themselves and those around them, we hope we're giving girls some of the tools necessary to combat that anxiety and darkness.

We hope that *A Girl Like You* gives parents, teachers, and all caregivers help in starting important discussions. From persevering through failure, pursuing one's passions, or learning that true beauty lies in one's actions, these messages are meant to spark conversations that ignite the understanding in girls that they are unstoppable. The world needs a girl—caring and strong, bold and brave—to be unstoppable. Now more than ever.

– Frank and Carla Murphy

Writing Activity

The beauty your actions and words bring to the world will be remembered by people. And you'll remember the people who did helpful and kind things for you. How many examples of kindness can you find in this book? What similar acts have you done for other people—or have other people done for you? Consider creating a gratitude journal. Draw and write about the helpful and kind things people have done for you. Don't forget to be thankful for the opportunities you've had to do the same for others. You can also record the things (big and little!) in your own life that you're thankful for, from family members and friends to favorite foods and hobbies. Gratitude is a powerful feeling to have—it builds awareness of all the ways people are helpful and kind, and it strengthens feelings of happiness and love. See if you can record three things in your gratitude journal everyday. Write on!